Death Comes Calling

Nicola Goumas

Death Comes Calling

MILTON & HUGO L.L.C.
4407 Park Ave., Suite 5
Union City, NJ 07087, USA

Website: *www. miltonandhugo.com*
Hotline: *1- 888-778-0033*
Email: *info@miltonandhugo.com*

Ordering Information:
Quantity sales. Special discounts are available on quantity purchases by corporations, associations, and others. For details, contact the publisher at the address above.

Library of Congress Control Number: 2024906503
ISBN-13:   979-8-89285-065-0   [Paperback Edition]
    979-8-89285-064-3   [Digital Edition]

Rev. date: 03/06/2024

CHAPTER ONE

The Visit

I'm sure you have a lot of questions about what has been happening recently.

I promise, I can explain.

The last two years of my life have been completely static. I have the same job that I've always had; a job that promises promotions that I never receive. The pay is still enough to get me by. It's predictable, and I've learned all that I can learn about it. It's emergency nursing, but somehow, I'm still not surprised by anything I see. I wake up at the same time every morning and report in for shift change. I take over my charges and go along with it, every day. There is the typical work team, the same people I've worked with for years. The coworkers that like to gossip, the coworkers that are quiet, the coworkers that become your best friends. Olivia is still my best work friend throughout all these years. The friendship is surface level but, at these times, that's all I can ask for. I don't have the emotional capacity to be a good friend right now. Maybe I should just get a dog.

I struggle to feel anything as deeply as I once did. I used to be so full of life. I feel happy at times, I feel sad at times, but mostly, I feel detached from everything I used to love. Every day I work under these fluorescent lights, and shiver in the cold halls of this hospital waiting to get home. Only to find myself feeling as unsettled and cold as I do in the hospital.

The break room provides no escape. I sit on the metal chairs and force conversation with my coworkers. Olivia is the gossiping coworker. She is not a malicious gossip. She usually shares positive updates, with only occasional negativity. Olivia can entertain for these long twelve hour shifts. From morning to evening, I don't feel as lonely at work as I do at home because of her. Olivia tells me the news of other coworkers, past and present. She is friends with everyone, and everyone confides in Olivia. It's almost like they feel so warm talking to her at the moment, they forget that nothing is kept private.

"How is Katie doing lately? I haven't talked with her since the Christmas party a year ago," Olivia questioned.

Tight lipped, I replied "You know Katie, same old, same old. I'm actually going to visit with her next week. I took PTO to spend some time with her."

The next week, I would spend with Katie was not a visit for pleasure. As always, she struggles with her boyfriend, Brandon. I try to check in with Katie, but everytime she picks up the phone, which is rare, it's almost like she is whispering on the other end. Katie assures me everything is fine and she is doing well. Fine people don't whisper into the phone with their best friend.

The silence is painful, since Katie and I have been friends since the fourth grade. Katie is one of the most secure people I know. Still, she needs constant reassurance. I don't mind being that person for her, she is a sister to me. It's my honor to be there when she needs a friend. Brandon has been Katie's longtime boyfriend. Brandon convinced Katie to move two hours away. I'm sure, to get her away from anyone that would support her. The reason, I think, is because of the drunken night they had a year ago. The local bar, ever the source of drama, was the last place most people saw Brandon and Katie. I was there, too.

In a fog of secondhand smoke, the three of us casually drank, to loosen up after our work week. Brandon, of course, was not casually drinking. Brandon, drinking his blue mixed drink, made derogatory comments toward an ex-girlfriend of his, who was minding her own business, at the other end of the bar. Katie giggled along, which was so out of character for sweet Katie.

"Sounds like you don't like to see your ex doing so well after leaving you, Brandon," I snarked.

Brandon erupted on me. All I could do was laugh at his tantrum. He was childish, unable to control himself, blue mouth and all. He looked like a toddler that had dropped his blue lollipop and was having a consequential meltdown. His cheeks flushed with anger and his hands started to shake. It was humorous to me, I smiled and excused myself from the bar. When I left, I saw Katie's reaction. Her face looked like she had just seen a ghost. She was petrified, it was like she wanted to scream for help, but just couldn't. I should've taken Katie with me.

Later that night, I was on my couch when I saw Katie was calling my phone. She never called me anymore. I fumbled my phone, trying to pick up as quickly as I could, but already my hands were sweating with the fear I had now sitting in my stomach. There was yelling and then a rustled disconnection. I called back countless times, as I was driving to the bar. Her car was not there anymore. I called again and again, driving to look for her at her home, where all the lights were on. I could hear both of them screaming inside. I honked once in the driveway, and Katie bursted through the door and came running to my car. Brandon ran after her, in his boxers, still blue mouthed, sobbing and screaming at her. He had something in his hand, but I was backing up so quickly, I didn't want to take the time to see what it was.

Katie was silent. Staring forward for a few minutes.

"Katie, what happened?" I asked as if I didn't know.

It was like Katie finally realized she was safe. She started crying so hard she couldn't catch her breath. I turned my interior lights on, and glanced at her. Her wavy brown hair was ratted. It was hard to see in the shadow cast by the light, but she had a swollen lump forming below the hollow of her cheek. I turned the lights off again, and continued driving.

"Did he do that to your jaw? That redness?"

She didn't answer. She didn't need to answer. I took Katie to my house. She slinked into the guest room and I heard nothing more from her that night. She left in the morning before I had woken up. She gave me a letter on the pillow. Katie wrote that she took a new job and she was moving with Brandon to another city, two hours from where we grew up. I was horrified, but it did not come as any news to me.

I would visit Katie at her new house a few times, in the past year. Always the same. It was like she was acting. We have such a deep bond, we both knew it was just a character she was playing to keep herself safe. Brandon loomed around, always just cutting his eyes at me, never speaking to me. On one of the visits, I was looking at their bookshelf, curious if Brandon could even read. There was a gun, somewhat hidden on top of the books. I realized then, Brandon had come out of the house that night with a gun in his hand. Had he tried to kill Katie? Had he tried to kill me? A question I did not want, or need, the answer to. I pretended not to see the gun even though I felt even more unsafe there, now. When I left that day, I decided I would not return again.

Until Katie called. I was working when my phone rang, so I kept the conversation short.

"I'm ready. I need you to help me," Katie said without even saying hello.

The wave of relief I felt was like taking my first breath. The weight lifted from me.

I told Katie, "I'm glad you called. I can take the week off soon, I'll help you move."

"I'm not moving, why would I move?"

"I just, thought-"

"No, I'm comfortable right where I'm at, I'll break the news to Brandon and he'll have to leave."

I had never heard Katie so self-assured. I was shocked, honestly. Katie, while amazing to me, had never been exceptionally...anything. She is average in most ways.

She is smart, but not a genius. She is beautiful but very unconventional. Katie has always felt like my little sister. I always needed to care for her and protect her from the world because of her innocent nature.

This change made me very curious. Katie seemed certain, without my encouragement or support. She sounded independent and unafraid of Brandon's abuse. I scheduled my time off two weeks in advance, and prepared for my week's stay. This trip would prove to be tense and a bit scary, I was sure.

CHAPTER TWO
Uninvited

I arrived at Katie and Brandon's house. Where there was usually overgrowth and weeds, there were beds of lavender, thistle, and deep purple violets. It was late in the season, maybe Katie took up a new gardening hobby. I arrived in the late morning, the porch light was still on. I thought Katie must not be awake yet. She knew of my arrival. I hoped Brandon wouldn't be too angry to be woken up by me at the door. I knocked softly, hoping to not trigger Brandon's tantrums, he already loathed me enough. I could only imagine his rage to find me on the porch, ready to move his things out.

I heard a dog barking on the other side of the door. The hair stood on the back of my neck. After obviously being in an abusive relationship that ended two years ago, I knew what the dog meant. A couple that is in dire straits, always, always, gets a dog. Most abusers think that adopting a dog is enough emotional leverage to further tie their victims to them. To prevent them from leaving.

My stomach sank, thinking that Katie has once again been convinced to stay from the time that she called me to come. Maybe she thought it would get better because they have a dog now. What nonsense would she believe this time?

Light footsteps approached the door. Katie opened the door and gestured the giant dog to the couch.

"Comet, everything's ok buddy! Go lay down." Katie smiled.

The dog obeyed and laid down quietly. Katie gave me the tightest hug. The first time we'd hugged in my recent memories.

Katie stepped back, "Oh my god, I'm so excited to see you! Try the new doorbell, it sounds so cute."

"The...doorbell?" Confused, I hit the doorbell. It *was* cute. It sounded like bells chiming in the happiest rhythm. I was taken aback at her demeanor. She was the Katie that I knew in college, again, the Katie that wasn't weighed down by depression. I looked her over, nonchalantly. Katie was dressed in trendy clothes, her hair was washed and styled. She even put on a little bit of makeup. She was warm and inviting. She normally looked like she was always waiting for a tragedy.

Katie said, "Come on, let's go get a bite to eat for brunch! What's up, how are you lately"

"What's up? What do you mean? What's up with you? Where is Brandon?-"

"I broke it off the day I asked you to come, I didn't want to wait anymore, and the timing was just right. So I went with it. Everything is fine now, let go-"

"Katie, no. I'm not going to lunch, I'm a little shell shocked at the moment can we go inside?"

"Umm..." she hesitated, glancing behind herself, "of course, sure! I can serve up some snacks while we catch up. I feel like I haven't *actually* been able to talk to you for years."

I felt the same way. As happy as I was to see Katie thriving, after what should've been a horrible break-up, something just didn't feel right. Her house smells wonderful, like she had just lit candles. And Katie, usually a bit of a messy person, looked like she had cleaned and organized. Not a trace of Brandon ever living in the house. Katie rushed off to the kitchen where I heard her making some food. It was beautiful, but I felt like I was in a stranger's home for the first time. Uneasy, I sat down in the sterile feeling living room. I looked around at all the same decor she had before, the same furniture, but it seemed almost creepy, as I waited alone.

My eyes moved around the room, "It looks great in here," I awkwardly shouted to her, "and... you got a dog?"

Katie rounded the corner with a charcuterie board handmade in minutes.

"Yeah! Isn't he wonderful! He is so peaceful, his name's Comet."

He wasn't wonderful, he was a big, shaggy black dog that left hair all over her white canvas couch. It was better than the blue curacao stains Brandon left, I suppose. Comet just looked at me. Not aggressively, but friendly as he sighed and laid his head on his paws. He begged to lay on my lap but I brushed him off, as I reached for the snacks. I picked up the decorative rosemary off the board and studied it, trying to think of something to say. I noticed artwork that looked new, a figurine sitting on the coffee table. It was beautifully crafted. All white stone, carved into a woman wearing a loose billowing dress. Three moons were carved in the base with a word I couldn't read, the artist's signature, probably.

"Wow, that's really cool," I pointed to the statue.

"Thanks. I got it at this shop on Meridian Avenue. Have you seen Meridian Avenue recently? There's so much construction! They're putting in a new boutique. I really want to go when it's finished. We can go to all the restaurants that are new while you're here. You'll love this one that has-"

I interrupted Katie. "So...sorry. Let's plan all of the fun stuff later."

Katie readjusted in her chair. She was suddenly as uncomfortable as I was. It was like she had been called into the principal's office, looking down at her pants and picking at the seam.

"I didn't expect Brandon to be gone today. I sort of expected to be in a fight by now," I laughed off the tension, "and I really didn't expect you to be doing so... well. Please, don't that the wrong way."

"Oh, I don't take that the wrong way, it just means my efforts are working! I took up some new hobbies last week, did you see the flower beds?"

"Yeah, really beautiful, Katie. Brandon isn't like... buried under the lavender bushes, right?" I joked, even though it was clear Katie was avoiding this conversation at every chance.

"You know, I could never. I just let people like that destroy themselves. I have no need to take revenge. He will be his own demise."

I couldn't argue with that. Katie is right, I always have loosely believed in karma, or at least something like it. I think that after Brandon proved to be a monster, anyone would wish hell upon him. But apparently not Katie. I guess she really was done. No hating Brandon, no missing Brandon, no loving Brandon, just acceptance. I felt better to know that. But I wasn't completely at ease.

I snuck Comet a piece of prosciutto as Katie told me how Comet came into her life at exactly the right time. As she talked, I was amazed at how Comet swallowed pieces of meat in an instant. He was a large dog, and he wasted no time on chewing.

Katie told me that she had decided that she finally had the courage to leave Brandon. But she wanted some alone time to process her emotions and find the strength to follow through. She started a hobby she could do alone to find some sort of meditation in the stress that was overwhelming. She had just finished putting her new flowers in the ground when the lonely, dirty dog approached her. Katie, a little hesitant of dogs, after we were chased on our bike too many times growing up, froze at the sight of Comet. She said Comet had such a calm presence that she extended her hand and he almost bowed to her. She said he had the most soulful eyes and they just looked at each other for a moment. Comet then rose to attention and walked to her front door and sat. Like he was waiting for her to let him in. She put her tools away and returned to the front yard to find Comet still sitting by the door. She said "I guess he just decided he was coming in."

Comet stood as she approached the door and nudged his head under her hand, to be pet by Katie. Katie realized her porch light had been left on, again, so she opened the door to turn off the switch. That's when Comet pushed past Katie, and ran into the house. Such a calm dog had immediately turned vigilant. Katie ran inside after the dog to find him barking and clawing at the closed bedroom door, where Brandon was taking his daily afternoon nap. Katie sank knowing how angry Brandon would be to be woken up by a stray dog inside the house.

Brandon ripped the door open and attempted to scream at Katie. When he saw the massive black dog snarling at him, Brandon's voice shook with anger when he asked Katie what the hell she was thinking. An intense argument broke out between the two and the dog stood in the middle, trying to separate Brandon from Katie.

As Brandon was screaming at Katie to get rid of the dog, Comet growled and even took a few snaps at his hands. But Katie surprisingly stood up for herself and told Brandon no. That she would not be getting rid of the dog, and in fact, he was the one that needed to leave.

I listened to this story so intently, Katie took a bite into another cube of cheese and Comet curled into her lap.

"Yeah, and then Brandon left for good!" Katie said, patting Comet's head.

"Wait, just like that? Katie, he abused you for years and he left that easily? There's no way. I don't believe it. Either there's more to the story or he is planning something bad. Abusers never just leave after being told to leave."

"No seriously, I haven't heard from him. I left all of his things outside and he must've already picked them up. He won't be back."

"How can you be so sure? Katie, I've been through this, this isn't normal."

"I'm positive, 100% sure he will not be back," Katie gave a satisfied smile and changed the subject.

Katie started to talk about the fun things we could do while I was visiting. But I couldn't pay attention. I knew Brandon would come back. And he would come back with a vengeance. I zoned out, looking at the clipping of rosemary I twirled in my fingers.

Katie snapped her fingers to pull me from my thoughts, "It's fine, snap out of it. Neither one of us is in any danger at all."

Katie went on to tell me of her promotion at work. We are both nurses, and she has been promoted to the director of nursing over the local hospital. I was so impressed. Of course, she is more than capable, but typically, those jobs are for twenty and thirty year veterans in nursing. We graduated from nursing school together only seven years ago. I congratulated Katie and we celebrated with a bottle of wine.

The day went on, and the wine went on, delightfully forgetting that I was still suspicious of the surely incoming Brandon. We watched our favorite TV series and laid on the couch, cuddling Comet. The lights dimmed and we all drifted to a nice, heavy sleep there, in the living room.

I jerked awake to Altiz jumping from the couch barking like mad. I dizzily rose and so did Katie. I'm sure the look on my face showed my fear. Katie, looking frustrated, tossed the blanket off herself, and got up, bumping around the living room. She went to the light switch by the door and turned on the porch light.

"Katie stop, I think someone's here. Didn't Brandon have a gun here?" I whispered through the constant barking.

"Oh that thing? No, I put it in a box with the rest of his stuff."

Oh, wonderful, I thought to myself. *This was it. Brandon was going to come in and shoot us. I hadn't heard any noises through the dog barking. But the way he barked at the door, I knew someone was out there.*

Katie went around to all the rooms, peering through the windows. Then, a gentle knock at the door, I could barely hear through the growls of Comet. I don't think I've ever been so scared. It had to be two, maybe three in the morning. I scrambled to get down behind the couch, to not be seen.

"Get down, hide!" I whispered, waving widely at Katie.

Katie smirked and walked quickly to the door. This was the strangest sight. While I, nearly pissing my pants, hid from a probable murderer, Katie boldly goes to answer the door? Has she lost her mind? She was the one protecting me now?

Katie approached Comet and told him "everything is ok, go sit."

What in the world is going on? I am speechless and afraid. For years, I had to hide my fear of Brandon so I could be strong for Katie. Hiding my fear had come to an end in seconds before Katie opened the door. I started to silently cry, gripping onto Comet for comfort. Katie was about to get us both killed.

I felt like I was standing outside of myself watching Katie open the door. It was Brandon. I flinched back under the cover of the couch. I expected to hear him yelling, or hear him push his way inside. When I heard nothing, I rose over the couch to see. Brandon looked different. He looked skinny and pale, almost blue. Maybe it was the glaring porch light washing out his complexion. Brandon looked wild with stress. I guess if I had lost a great person like Katie, I would be a wreck as well. When I peeked to see Brandon's face, he looked desperate. He didn't look angry or violent, like I had expected. I watched, hoping he wouldn't see me hiding from him.

"Well hello, I really didn't expect you." Katie sounded annoyed.

"What is going on?" Brandon said. His words were jarring.

"Well, we're just were having a glass of wine to celebrate my promotion-"

"Katie. What is happening? Look at me-"

"That's enough of your hysterics, Brandon. It's time for you to go home."

Katie tried to shut the door when Brandon hand slammed onto the door to stop her.

"No I-" Brandon stuttered as Katie gestured toward Comet, who rose from his spot on the couch.

Brandon noticed Comet, turned and stumbled off. I watched him through the window as he got in his car and started crying and pulling at his greasy black hair. I had never seen Brandon act like this. Katie seemed to have complete control over this whole disturbance. Brandon looked scared and confused as the porch light faded from his face while he was backing out of the drive.

"We should call the police-" I said with so much panic. Katie could see how terrified and confused I was.

"Absolutely not, they would just ignore it and tell us we were crazy," Katie calmly said to me and she sat down and put her arms around me. She hugged me for a few minutes and said she was going to her bed.

I was so upset that I couldn't sleep the rest of the night. As I laid on her couch, looking out the front window, I watched the sun come up. Katie slept while I went to the kitchen to make coffee for the two of us. I sat the cups at the table and waited. I was about to have a long, clear, conversation with Katie. There was something she was not telling me.

CHAPTER THREE

Just a Few More Days

I waited for Katie that morning. I decided to take a shower and freshen up before the day started. I couldn't help but feel on edge. I was starting to feel a little afraid of Katie. I didn't think she had done anything wrong, but she was feeling less familiar to me. She used to be so steady but now she was unpredictable and that scared me.

Katie and I knew everything about each other. We shared every milestone, every celebration, and every sadness throughout our lives. Every dark secret we could ever have, the other held the key to. But I felt, at this time, Katie was keeping something from me. It made me feel like an outsider in her life now. Paired with the events of the night before, I just wanted to know I was alone, for a moment, in the bathroom to sort out the new fears I had about my stay with Katie.

Comet tried to enter the bathroom after me, but I shooed him away. As I locked the door and turned to brush my teeth, I heard a heavy bump against the door. Surely, it was the clingy dog wanting to accompany me. I took a deep, tired breath and continued. I turned the sink faucet on, to the hottest temperature. I waited for it to get warm, but it never did. The color was so clear and blue. It was freezing, I had hoped the shower would be warmer. I took off my day-old clothes and turned the squeaky handle on the shower. It was a bit warmer but still uncomfortable. I thought maybe Katie was having problems with the water heater. I bore the chilly shower. As I was showering I could hear Katie singing in the other room. It was refreshing to know she had woken up in a cheerful mood. I couldn't make out the song, but it sounded like an old song. I didn't realize she could sing so well, it sounded so effortless and light.

I got out of the chilly shower and wrapped a towel around myself for warmth. I shivered and cleared the mirror. I heard something bump again. It was above me this time. I knew it could not be the dog this time. It was heavier than him anyhow. Just a single bump. I froze to listen closer but when I heard nothing else, I scrambled to throw my clothes on and leave the bathroom quickly. I felt rushed to leave the bathroom and my anxiety made the walls close in.

I thought Katie had possibly been knocking to use the restroom but I went to her bedroom, I found her asleep, snoring with her mouth open. I was sure I had heard her singing. If not Katie, then maybe it was a neighbor walking by singing, or a radio alarm, or maybe my hearing was distorted by the shower and I had heard nothing at all.

I thought, while Katie's sleeping, I'll just take a look around. I was trying to find the source of the singing. I walked through her house, eyes following me. I think I felt this way because Comet followed behind me to every room I entered.

I went to the bookshelf to see if Brandon had really taken the gun with him. If he didn't, that could explain Katie's inexplicable confidence last night. I looked through the books and didn't find his gun. Which wasn't comforting, not that I anticipated feeling any comfort for the next few days at Katie's house.

She had some books that still had the sales stickers on the spines. They were brand new. I skimmed some of the books, until I picked up an unassuming plain book. It was a thin, hard backed book. It was heavier than I expected, it almost fell from my hands. There was no title, and no cover art, just a plain black book. I figured it may have been Katie's journal, so I put it away to respect her privacy.

As I was shoving the book back into its space, a rustle came from the hall. I looked to see nothing except the hallway light on, that I was sure I had turned off. Again, I felt rushed to leave the room.

I sought peace in the kitchen. I sat down alone at the table but still felt like something was hanging over me. I wanted something to distract me from the feeling of something creeping behind my back. I decided I would see if her water heater was working properly so she could have a warm shower when she woke up. The basement door sat in the dark corner of the kitchen. Somehow, even with the sun up, the corner seemed darker than it should've been. I reached for the doorknob, and Comet jerked his attention from me, to the other direction. Now, looking into the living room, he sat like he was carved out of stone, as if someone was dangling a treat to him. I said his name, and it was like I wasn't even present to him. I ignored his change in posture. I continued to turn the knob on the old wooden door.

I went down the stairs, which felt like they were fragile and worn from age. The air was dense and hazy from the dust I had stirred. Regardless, the basement smelled like fresh lavender and rosemary. I tried the light switch at the bottom of the stairs. Apparently, this was the only place in the house the lights would not turn on. I rustled to get my phone's flashlight out of my pocket.

I took a look around squinting from the fluorescent light from my phone. I found the water heater in the corner. I touched the outside of the tank and it was very warm. Nothing looked or seemed out of order with the water heater so I made my way back to the stairs, this time looking a little slower around the basement. Cardboard boxes lined the cement walls. Trying my hardest not to be nosy, I caught the writing on a few. It looked like a different language was written on some of them. Sure, there were normal ones, like "old clothes," "books," "photos," but some of them just looked like hand written symbols on the faces of the boxes. The other legible boxes were labeled with black marker, but these symbols on the others were written in a different type of marker. It looked like the ink had become clumpy then dried out into a flakey crust. I brushed some of the flakes off the writing and saw under the crust, the box was stained with the ink. The stain of the symbol was deep red, not black. I wiped my hand off on my jeans, but the dark rusty color stayed on my fingers.

I hurried up the stairs, remembering the childhood memory of running up the stairs from a dark basement. The feeling that something would reach out and grab you if you weren't quick enough. I didn't run, even though I wanted to, so I kept my eyes on the door and told myself that nothing was going to grab me from below. It felt a bit silly once I crossed the threshold into the kitchen to see Katie's bright face pouring the coffee I had made.

"Why were you in my basement?" Katie lowered her eyebrows and her brightness dulled into suspicion.

"The shower was cold this morning, I thought there may have been a problem with the water heater." I said. I wanted to ask her about the boxes but didn't.

Katie said there was nothing wrong with it, and that the water in the kitchen was warm. She turned on the faucet briefly, to show me the steam rising from the sink basin. I tilted my head and stared in silent disbelief. Katie sat down and patted the other chair for me to sit, smiling. I sat with her, kind of glad to not feel alone in the house anymore.

"So what will we do today? I'll look online if there's anything that catches your interest."

"Well actually, before we do that, can I talk to you about something?" I gently asked.

"Sure, anything. You look like something is bothering you-"

I looked down, "Well, yes. I don't want to be critical of the way you're handling your separation. Everyone deals with trauma differently. But, Katie, I just feel...I don't know...*off* about everything that happened last night. We have a few more days left of my visit with you. I don't want to feel this tension for the remainder of the week. Please, tell me what's going on."

Katie swallowed hard. It seemed like finally she had shown a glimpse of insecurity. She looked around and asked, "Promise me, this stays between us, don't go telling anyone, especially Olivia," she said with a serious tone.

I promised.

Katie explained "So..." she sighed,

"Do you remember when my grandma passed away, and I got a lot of boxes from her house? I told Brandon about all the beautiful knick-knacks and jewelry and books that I inherited from her. Well, when Brandon needed money for his new video game console, he pawned the jewelry behind my back. The only necklace I had left was one the pawn shop wouldn't buy. He told me it was cheap and so ugly a pawn shop wouldn't even take it."

Katie lowered the collar of her shirt to show me the necklace she was talking about. It was on a dingy leather cord, with three moons, two crescents on each side of a full moon. You could see the rough tool marks in the silver colored metal, left by the maker. It had the three purple stones in it, too. It was pretty plain, but she clearly loved it.

Katie continued, "I began to cry that he would not only sell what I had left of my grandma, but then insult the jewelry she left for me. I argued with him about his disrespect. He took a box from the stack that was still left in the living room and put it in the front yard and burned it in front of me. I watched all of my grandma's memories being taken from me, by this psychopath. I fell to my knees realizing how cruel he can be when I challenged him. After he shoved past me, I put the box out with the hose. But, when I went to clear the ashes off, I picked up a book that didn't burn. It didn't even have a mark on it. I brushed the soot off the cover to see what it was. But there wasn't a title, it was a blank black book with blank pages. And I thought it was impossible that it didn't burn. I brought it inside and kept it on my shelf. I stared at it for weeks, wondering why my grandma would pass a blank book on to me. When the grief wasn't as strong anymore, I thought it would be sweet and sentimental to use it as a journal. I moved the book to my nightstand so I could vent my feelings, for once. I wrote it all out and tucked it away under the mattress when Brandon was sleeping. I wrote about how much I actually hated Brandon. How much I wished something or someone would save me from this life I was living. I woke up before Brandon the next morning and I went to throw away the pages because I was scared Brandon would find it and be mad. But when I looked, it was empty. My words were completely gone. It was an empty book again. I rushed it out of the bedroom and flicked through every page. I thought 'what happened' I knew I had written in this just the night before, I thought I had gone crazy. I heard Brandon waking up, so I put it in the bookshelf. Brandon rubbed his eyes as he entered the living room. I looked at him expecting his usual negativity. Brandon looked up and started to insult the way I look in the morning when he stopped abruptly and got wide eyed. He rushed into the bathroom and vomited. I went in after him and he waved me out of the room. Before I left, I saw him vomiting, like, black sludge or something. It was so disgusting I almost vomited myself. When Brandon finally came out to the kitchen he looked so white and like all the color in his face was drained. He had these blue bags under his eyes like he hadn't slept in a week. I asked him if he was ok but he just got sarcastic with me so I left him alone. He turned on the sink and got a glass of water. That's when we both heard the house groan and rumble. We looked at each other to confirm that it was real. We both kind of froze for a second and Brandon went to the window to see if there was a storm coming in. But it was clear, by the time he pulled away from the window, it was quiet again. For a few more weeks, the house made more new and alarming noises. I called a repairman but nothing was wrong. I called an electrician about the lights always turning on but the wiring was fine too. Brandon got sicker and sicker, too. I would see him shivering. I thought it would be the Flu, but I never got sick, I actually was feeling better than ever.

That's when I started working out again, and taking up my hobbies again. I felt a little guilty that I was feeling energetic and motivated, and Brandon was slowly deteriorating. He still wouldn't go to see a doctor even though he was getting worse.

Since I was feeling so brand new, I thought I would organize and get rid of some of the hoarded stuff around the house before the winter. So I started with the basement. When I got to my grandma's old boxes, I started to get curious about what these knick-knacks were, why were they given to me? They seemed like handmade crafts. I started looking up to see if they were trendy things to make back in the day, but they weren't. I found nothing similar. So I started to look up the symbols on them. They were symbols of a deity. I read and learned all I could of this deity that must've meant so much to my grandma. And I thought it was cool, so I started making my own symbols and decorating around the house with them so I could feel a little more connected to my grandma since I missed her so much. That's when the house went from bad to worse. It made so much noise in the night it was almost violent, we were constantly awoken by doors opening, lights turning on, we heard a woman singing in the night so many times. While I wasn't afraid, Brandon insisted we looked for a new house, he really thought this house was haunted. And to make a really long story short, I invited something in when I looked into my grandmother's stuff. And it did NOT like Brandon. I continued to read more about this deity that my grandma worshiped. The deity would help your life become what you wanted it to be. And it helps that this deity is the protector of women, the guiding light in the dark. After I wrote in that journal, I think I invoked the deity. These websites said after you come to her with your problems and woes, the deity would leave behind an invitation, in order to initiate the work she would do. The invitation comes in the form of her beloved dog companions. You wouldn't believe, shortly after, Comet showed up to me. I knew I had to accept him to initiate her help. And Brandon began to get weaker and weaker. He didn't have power over me anymore. Did you see the way Brandon looked last night? That's because I invited this to happen."

Katie waited for my response. I was trying to put my thoughts into words in a way that wouldn't offend her. Katie was not doing as well as she seemed. I expected something of a mental break to happen after such a bad relationship, but this was delusional.

"Katie, you know I love you. But do you know how all of this sounds? This sounds…I'm sorry. I don't want to be harsh, but I think you're thinking too far into these coincidences."

Katie smirked arrogantly, "I know you can feel the house. You've probably heard these things too. I don't want you to be afraid or anything, there's really nothing to be scared of. It'll go away soon, I think."

I really didn't want to be validated in my paranoia about the creepy sounds I had heard. I refuse to believe this was some kind of haunting in the house. Katie was stubborn about this and clearly wasn't going to hear reason. So I said we would pick the conversation up another time, and suggested we go for breakfast. The day went on with window shopping and a trip to an art museum. I was thinking of so many things to do and places to go because I did not want to be in that house anymore.

When we returned, we took to the living room couch to unwind. The noises continued after Katie left for her bed. It sounded like there was something there that was too big to fit in the house and the walls were trying to hold together. I told myself it was all in my head. I tried to convince myself the weight I felt was self-imposed anxiety after hearing such a disturbed ghost story from my friend. In the dimly lit living room, I sat with Comet trying to sleep. "Just a few more days," I told myself. I would leave now, but Katie still clearly needed the company. I couldn't just abandon my friend in such a time of mental distress.

After a few more uncomfortable days went on, I invited Katie to come and stay at my house. She declined saying she would be ok and that she had to stay home to take care of her dog. I was still afraid that Brandon had lost his mind too. I feared Brandon would somehow know Katie's vulnerable mental state and plan to return to harm her or even try to win her back. But, it was time for me to leave and go home to my boring life. And try to forget the week I just endured. As Katie and I hugged goodbye, she said quietly into my ear "I know you can relate to all of this. You don't have to keep living in the pain from the past." I looked at her without expression and turned to leave.

CHAPTER FOUR

Leave the Lights On

When I arrived home, I thought I would feel better. The rural quiet town didn't feel as welcoming as it always did. I drove through the empty highway of wilted grass and bare trees. I arrived in the gravel drive of my hundred year old farm house. Of course, I didn't use it as a farm, but the antique charm made the house feel lived in and cozy.

Winter was approaching quickly, so it had been a few weeks since I'd been out into the woods surrounding my house. I usually go out so often that I've unintentionally made my own trails. One trail led to my creek. I've never told anyone about my creek. It's like my own private retreat, the only place on earth that no one knows is there. The creek is hidden between two wooded hills and is usually canopied by beautiful sycamore and maple trees. But this time of year, the leaves have fallen and the coldest air reaches onto the creek's shores. There was a long grass between the trees and the water. The white rock bedded in the water made the water run clear. In the middle of the shallow creek was the rock I sit on. I don't mind walking into the cold water to get to the rock. I'm not sure where the creek started, or where it ended, but sitting on the rock felt like there was no world outside of the water.

I turned my rusted key in the front door, to an empty house. My ears rang in the silence of my living room. Taking a deep sigh of relief, I looked the room over, glad to be in my own space, away from all of the stress.

The last two years, I've done so much work to clear the negativity out of my home that lingered after the breakup. I could ignore that I felt the house was a little emptier now. I would rather feel the emptiness I'm left with than the chaos it used to be.

I tossed and turned for hours trying to sleep the night I returned. I was worried for Katie. The story she told was very real to her. I shouldn't have invalidated her the way I did. She was going through a lot, I shouldn't have been so quick to judge. But I kept thinking of the things I heard at her house and all of the strange things that happened.

A knock broke the silence. I shot up and waited to see if it was a real knock and not my semi-sleep state. I looked out my living room window. I felt adrenaline rush through my body and settle in my stomach. I saw a man, back turned away from the front door. I recognized the body figure and gait, it was Brandon. He'd come to take his anger out on me, or interrogate me about Katie, I was sure. I stood on the other side of the front door, where he had knocked. He just stood there for a minute, then knocked again.

"I have a gun!" I shouted, hoping he would believe my lie.

"I don't blame you." He said quietly. His voice sounded raspy and weak.

Brandon's voice sounded like it was forced out, "I'm sorry for everything and listen, I really do understand if you don't want to forgive me. And I understand if you don't let me in-"

"Good, because I'm not doing either."

"Please, just tell me what's happening to me." Brandon started to cry.

I definitely wasn't letting him in. But, I was curious. I turned on the porch light and cracked the door open, leaving the chain lock latched.

"What are you talking about, Brandon? Haven't you bothered everyone enough? Why are you here at this time of the night?"

"I- I don't know," Brandon looked defeated. He said "I don't know what's happening to me. I haven't slept, everything I eat makes me sick. The doctors say my bloodwork is fine, but something is wrong."

"So, why are you here? Have you tried being sober, for once?"

Brandon lowered his head and sighed. This version of Brandon felt completely different. When he raised his head back up to look at me, I shuddered in disgust. He did look ill. An already slim man, looking like he had lost every bit of muscle and fat he had. His long black hair was sticking to his cool-pale skin with sweat and oil. The bags under his eyes were reaching down to his protruding cheek bones. And his mouth. His gums, blue-ish gray and his teeth looked rotted, and he smelled rancid. I was stunned. In all my time taking care of patients in the emergency room, I had never seen anything like this.

My skin crawled looking at him, and he noticed the expression on my face as I stared at him.

"*This* is what I'm talking about. I just want to know what's happening."

"Well, Brandon, I'm only a nurse. I'm not a doctor. I'm not qualified to-"

"Not your professional opinion. What did Katie do to me?"

"Katie would never hurt anyone and you know that! I don't like you coming to my house, this late especially, to talk so poorly of her, after everything you've done."

"Didn't she tell you anything? Did she say she poisoned me? Or slipped me some medication from the hospital or something?"

"I just told you, she would never do something like that. Get off my porch, and if you come back, I'm calling the police."

I shut the door and saw him wobble to his car. He was hunchbacked and it looked like he was in pain from the short walk to the driveway. His knees were giving out as he was getting into the driver's side door. I saw his taillights disappear into the dark where he turned onto the highway. I didn't know why he would come here, we mutually hate each other. Maybe he's gotten into more serious substances than alcohol.

I turned off the porch light and got back into my bed, knowing I wouldn't close my eyes the rest of the night. I stared at the ceiling, wondering what was really going on. He's clearly sick. I knew for certain Kaite was not capable of any of the accused potential causes Brandon had asked about. The image of Brandon I had just seen would not leave my mind. He looked like he was inches from death, if not already beyond it. He looked vile.

A louder knock at the front door broke the silence. I threw my blankets onto the floor and stomped to the door, angry that Brandon had come back. The porch light was shining brightly, even after I knew I had turned it off. I yanked the front door open so hard it left a crack on the wall behind it and yelled out "I'm calling the police! Brandon, leave me alone!" I stared into the dark abyss of my front yard. I squinted to see any sign of movement. The cold air made me clutch my robe to my chest. I stood there, breathing rapidly, as my foggy exhales impaired my sight. There was no sound, not even any wind. I knew I would not get any rest unless I made sure Brandon had actually left.

I stepped off my porch and tiptoed around my house. The leaves crunched under my feet as I looked out. When I got to the back of my house, I looked into the woods. I saw no sign of anyone. I was beginning to think I had only dreamed of the knock and only imagined that I had turned the porch light off. I paused to collect my thoughts at the edge of the woods, looking out to my creek.

I turned to walk back to the front entry, but I saw something in the corner of my eye as I turned. I quickly looked back to my creek again holding my breath. It looked like a light, it looked like a glow from a candle.

I got closer, hiding as well as I could behind the trees I passed along the way. I saw no one there, and I didn't see a source of the light. The creek was bright from the reflection of the moon onto the white rocks. I took in the calm, and waded through the water to sit on the rock, where I always sit. I put my head in my hands and tears started rolling down my face.

After everything I've been through in the past, I had a habit of numbing myself and telling myself I was crazy so I didn't have to accept the world around me. But this is my safest place, it felt right to let go of all of my anxiety and stress that I had kept hidden. I didn't know what was real anymore, and I was afraid.

This made everything I had been through with Katie over the last week harder to grasp. I didn't know if any of it actually happened or if I misunderstood everything I had seen. I shook my head and stood up firmly.

"Of course it's not real." I reassured myself as I rubbed the ice cold tears off my cheeks.

When I stood up to cross the water, I could hear the bugs and frogs again. I didn't realize until I heard them, that the creek had been completely void of the sounds of the woods around it.

I returned to my bed. I'm not sure if I slept or not, but the morning came soon after I laid down.

I wanted my life back before I had gone to Katie's house. It was so boring and predictable, but at least I wasn't in perpetual confusion. As I thought about how I wanted to be bored once again, I second guessed myself. What I actually wanted was to be like I was years ago. Able to feel everything around me, to care about my friends and have a social life. I wanted to care about my job again, and I wanted my passion back. What had I become that I was so neutral and passive. The depression I have felt for so long had become who I was.

Four more days passed, and I was scrolling on my phone on my lunch break. I sat across from Olivia who was gossiping, despite my disengagement. I was half listening to her when I caught her saying Brandon's name.

"Wait a minute? Brandon? What about him?"

Olivia handed her phone, "Didn't you see this on the news? Brandon died."

CHAPTER FIVE

Retribution

I read the short obituary. It didn't mention any funeral services, not that I would've gone. As much as I hoped it was natural causes, the lump in my throat told me that there was nothing natural about his death.

"What happened? Do you know?" Olivia asked.

"No. I didn't know he passed." The room spun and Olivia's voice turned into humming in my ears. My eyes fell out of focus, I thought I would be sick.

After spending the next hour with my head on the desk in the nurses' station, I clocked out early.

Slamming my car's door shut I fumbled for my phone and called Katie in my dark car.

"Helloooo" Katie answered in a sing-song voice.

"What the hell happened to Brandon?" my voice shook in fear that Katie changed her tone.

"What do you mean?"

I reclined back in the seat "You haven't heard, yet…"

"Oh what, that he's dead? Yeah, I heard."

Katie didn't sound conflicted or grieving at all. She *had* to be in denial.

I spoke again through the awkward pause, "Are you ok? I'm sure you have a lot of mixed feelings. It's hard to lose someone that you were so close to for all those years, even if he treated you the way he did."

"To be honest, I saw it coming. You can't live your life that way without meeting an unsavory end." Katie said matter of fact.

"Unsavory end? The obituary didn't say how he died."

The line went quiet. I heard Katie let out a frustrated sigh.

Katie said, "I know, but I can only assume. I don't talk to anyone in his family anymore. I guess, I'll never know for sure what officially killed him."

Katie asserted that she was ok, and I said goodbye. *Officially* killed him? Katie was sounding less and less innocent.

I decided the next day, I decided I would have to get to the truth on my own. I went to the local police department to ask for a copy of the police report from Brandon's death.

It wasn't any easy to get them to make me a copy, the police were very apprehensive of releasing the report. But as with most public records, they could not deny my request. I sat on my bed to read it that night. The police report read:

"The emergency police line was contacted by *redacted*, a neighbor of the victim (Brandon Fisher) at 3:10 AM on November 20, 2023. *redacted* stated that she heard loud music coming from apartment 2. *redacted* knocked on the apartment belonging to Fisher and stated that she smelled smoke. *redacted* stated that when she knocked the music stopped and she could hear water running. *redacted* continued to knock to attempt to ask Fisher to keep quiet. *redacted* stated she noticed all lights were on through the crack of the door. She then heard multiple large dogs barking and snarling and grew concerned about the smell of smoke that was getting stronger. *redacted* then called the police after 10 minutes of attempted contact with Fisher.

When police arrived on scene at 3:15 AM, police were unable to make contact by knocking. Police noted the strong smell of smoke but did not hear the dogs inside. Due to the hazard of the smoke, police broke the door to make entry. Police searched the apartment. Contents of the apartment upon arrival, a mattress on the floor, a cardboard box used as a nightstand, fridge, oven, and molded food. No dogs or any other animals were inside the apartment at the time of entry. Fisher had no other belongings inside the apartment. Fisher was found, partially burned on his mattress. Cause of the fire has not been determined. No signs of forced entry and no signs of anyone exiting the apartment. Investigation will follow with Homicide Units and Fire Marshall. Photo evidence attached"

I finished reading the report and paused with my fingers on the edge of pages to continue. I wanted to see the photos, but I knew I would not be able to take back the images after I saw them. I held my breath and flipped the page over. The apartment looked like he only had one box of things he had taken when he left Katie's house. It was bare. Brandon laid, dead on his mattress, burned. His hair melted into globs of black sludge. His eyes burnt completely from his head, like pits. His hands were down to the bone. Still, large patches of blue skin on his torso, contrasted his burns. I wondered if the police had noticed at all, the bare mattress wasn't burnt at all. It was clean. I noticed something even more strange. The cardboard box beside him.

The box had some of those symbols on it. Katie must have used one of the boxes from her basement to pack his things in. I stashed the report away in my end table and I looked online to see what the symbol actually meant. It was a symbol of the deity she had told me about.

The caller said she was knocking because of the loud music. There was no radio, there was no TV, there was virtually nothing that could play music inside his apartment; he didn't even have a phone. And the police said there were no dogs in his apartment either. The caller could have mistaken the sounds coming from a different apartment. Coincidences happen all the time.

I wanted to see Katie as soon as possible. I texted her to tell her I was coming to her house on Saturday to talk about Brandon's horrific passing. She sent no response.

Saturday came, and I sped into her driveway and braked so hard I flung rocks into her grass. She came out, looking so well rested, and pleasantly surprised to see me. This time, Comet did not bark at me, he greeted me also. I was almost in a rage, Brandon had clearly been killed. The crime scene photos have played as a slideshow in my mind since I saw them. I was so haunted by his injuries. My distrust for Katie had driven me into a mental breakdown there in her quaint neighborhood. I screamed at her the moment I stepped out of my door, slamming it behind me. Katie rushed me inside her house under her arm.

Inside, I crossed my arms and told her everything the police report said. She looked surprised, I could tell this was something she hadn't expected.

"Katie, what in the hell is happening?" I cried and gasped between my words.

Katie hugged me, and comforted me. After a few minutes of calming me down, I took a deep breath and looked around. The house didn't have the same presence it did on my visit earlier. It felt airy, where before there was a nagging feeling of something watching.

Katie said to me, "It's hard to accept the reality that we cannot wish misfortune on those we really want to. It would be bad for our hearts. As much as I wanted Brandon out of my life, I didn't think this would be the result. But... a deal's a deal. I told you what I had done. I wanted him out of my life and I wanted to be on track again, like I had never even met Brandon. I wrote all of that out in that journal. That deity, the one I told you about, made it true. She sent me Comet as an invitation. I accepted him. She began to work in my house to make Brandon leave forever. If you stick around, you'll notice the sounds have stopped and the heaviness is gone. When Brandon died, the agreement was met. I now have the life I would've had if Brandon had never ruined it. It's like he never ever existed to me. I have my life back the way it was before Brandon took all the joy from me."

I remember feeling overwhelmed by Katie's explanation. I'm still not sure if it is real, but it's worth the chance. I wanted to be who I was before our breakup, I wanted to see colors as brightly as I once did. To experience the emotion from my favorite movies and songs. The paper you read this on, was ripped from the journal from Katie's house. I am trying to convince myself to feel remorse, but like with other emotions, I just can't feel as vividly anymore…yet. Maybe I am unremorseful because of my depression or maybe it's because I know that you deserve this. Either way, nothing can be done to reverse the sacrifice I've made; you for me.

Like I said in the beginning, I'm sure you had a lot of questions. I hoped this would explain what has been happening to you, Anthony. When you hear those bumps in the night, feel your body rotting inside itself, I want you to think of what you did to me. I want you to know what's calling to you, and I want you to know how it ends.